Lilian Finch, Her Maiden Voyage

Kelly Lin Roncace

Eloquent Books

Eloquent Books
An imprint of Strategic Book Group
P.O. Box 333
Durham CT 06422
www.StrategicBookGroup.com

ISBN 978-1-60860-796-9

Printed in the United States of America

Book Design/Layout by: Andrew Herzog

Dedication

In addition to my always supportive husband Jeff and ever inspiring daughter Rene', this book is dedicated to everyone who loves words and the magic they bring to our lives every day.

Contents

Book 1
Born a Pirate
7

Book 2
Kidnapped!
45

Book 3
Tragedy and Freedom
73

Book 1

Born a Pirate

"*There be no worse luck then havin' a fair one come aboard.*"

~ *unknown pirate, circa. 1919*

Chapter 1

"She's bleeding too much. We have to find a way to stop the bleeding or we're going to lose her."

The doctor worked frantically on the young woman who had just given birth. A nurse tended to the newborn, while the infant's father stood quietly in the corner, too frightened to move.

"Sir, the bleeding won't stop. Nothing I do will slow it down," said another nurse. After a long battle, the doctor finally stood and took a step back from the young mother who lay dying on her bed. He saw the life draining from her small body. The doctor glanced up at her husband, who was still standing stiffly in the corner of the bedroom.

"Mr. Finch? Would you like to come speak to your wife? I'm afraid it may be your last chance," the doctor said gently to the new father.

Henry Finch slowly approached the bed where his wife of three years lay clinging to her last breath. She looked pale, but just as beautiful as ever. He couldn't believe this lovely creature was near death.

He kneeled at her bedside and tenderly took her hand in his. Her tiny fingers were as cold as ice.

"Lilian? Lily, can you hear me?"

He spoke softly, choking back the fear in his voice.

"Lily, you can't leave me now. You can't leave us." He paused to look over his shoulder at the nurse holding his newborn child.

"She's a girl, sir. A healthy baby girl," the nurse told the frightened father.

"It's a girl, Lily. She's beautiful and healthy and I don't know how I'm going to be able to do this alone."

Lilian's eyes fluttered weakly and her lips parted slowly. She opened her eyes just enough to see Henry and she spoke very softly to him.

"Your love will guide you, Henry. And our love will live forever. I love you my darling. Tell her of me." Her final words faded away gently. She closed her eyes as she took one final breath, and then she lay lifeless in front of her adoring husband and tiny, newborn baby girl.

"Doctor," Henry whispered, turning hopelessly toward the doctor behind him, being careful not to let go of Lilian's hand.

The doctor ran to his patient and grabbed her free hand, placing his index and middle fingers together on her wrist. The doctor stood perfectly still for what seemed like an eternity. He gently lay Lilian's hand back down by her side.

"Doctor, is she..." Henry had trouble forming the words he needed to say. "Is she gone?"

The doctor nodded and placed a sympathetic hand on the young widower's shoulder.

Henry Finch, "Dead Eye" as he was known around the docks and aboard his ship, was not an emotional man. He rarely became sad or upset, and hadn't cried since he was an infant himself.

As he sat on the edge of the bed, staring down at his lifeless, but beautiful wife, a lump formed in his throat. It felt as if he was being strangled by some invisible being that had snuck up on him from behind. He felt his eyes burn and throb. Finally, tears formed in his sore eyes and he wept. The doctor and nurses left him and his wife alone in their room.

The nurse had wrapped the baby in a warm blanket and carried her along as they left the room.

Outside the door, the doctor turned to the nurse.

"We'll give him some time. When we feel he is ready, we'll take the baby to him."

"Aye, doctor," the nurse replied. There was a slight hint of worry in her voice.

Chapter 2

"Are you ready, sir?" the nurse asked Henry, as she prepared to pass the tiny, baby girl to her father. This would be his first time holding any baby at all, and it would be his own flesh and blood.

"Yes, ma'am, I believe I am," he answered, looking a bit nervous, but excited at the same time. "And all I must do is hold her head steady?"

"Aye, sir. Be sure to cup her tiny head in your hand, and the rest will just come to ye naturally."

The nurse bent down, cradling the baby in her arms. Henry held out his muscular hands. The baby girl transferred from the nurse's experienced hands to Henry's amateur mitts with ease and grace. Henry pulled the baby to his chest and stared into her deep, blue eyes.

"Her eyes are like the sea," he said. "She's as beautiful as her mother."

Henry, who had just lost the love of his life and taken on the challenges of parenthood all on his own, broke into a smile of sincere happiness. The baby, as if she knew this huge, rustic man was her daddy, cooed and seemed to smile right back at him.

"She seems to know you already, sir," the nurse noted.

"She does, doesn't she?" Henry said with pride. "She's amazing, and such a healthy, strong, little one already. She's smart, too!"

Father and daughter sat together and stared at one another for a long, restful time while the doctor and nurses gathered their belongings and made arrangements to have Henry's wife's body taken away.

When she had finished, the nurse who had first tended to the baby girl approached the small, but happy family.

"We're about finished here, sir," she told Henry.

"Thank you so much for everything," he said, attempting to rise from the chair while holding the baby.

"Please sir, don't bother. I can see you two are comfortable," she insisted, smiling at them both. "If I may, sir, have you decided what you're going to call her?"

Henry heard what the nurse said, but had been so overwhelmed with the emotions of the day that he had totally forgotten to chose a name for his new daughter. He looked down at the beautiful infant who was resting so peacefully in his arms. She looked up at him with those deep, sea-blue eyes. Suddenly, her name came to him as if delivered by angels.

"Her name will be Lilian just as her mother's. I'll even call her Lily on more informal occasions. Lilian Finch. At least her mother's name can live on in this little one's lively, little soul."

"I think her mother would be very happy and honored, sir," the nurse assured him. "It's a beautiful and strong name."

"Thank you, nurse," he said dreamily in reply, already back in the gaze of his new daughter Lilian. "And thank you Lilian, for being my beautiful baby girl."

Chapter 3

enry "Dead Eye" Finch had spent much of his life out to sea. He traveled the oceans in search of riches, treasure and, on occasion, a new ship for his crew. Henry "Dead Eye" Finch was indeed a pirate. He wasn't the most ruthless pirate on the seas, but he had his share of carefree moments and close calls.

Of all the challenges Henry had faced on the open sea, being a father was the toughest challenge of all. He wanted to raise his daughter on his own, but he didn't want to take her sailing on the ocean until she was a bit older. Not to mention, pirate lore said having a female on board, no matter what her age, was forbidden. Females, pirates believed, brought bad luck while aboard a sailing vessel. Therefore, Henry wasn't sure his crew would be in accord with him bringing young Lilian on board to sail with them.

For this reason, Henry had to make a serious, life-changing decision. He decided to disguise Lilian as a boy child right from the time of her birth. In private, he would treat her as a girl, and be sure she knew the ways of the women folk, but in order to someday have his daughter join him on the ocean, and for him to be able to go back to sailing – his life's passion and livelihood – he knew he would have to conceal her true identity.

While Lilian was an infant, passing her off as a little boy would be simple. He dressed her in boys' apparel. He kept her hair cut short once it started to grow. And he simply called her by their shared last name, Finch.

One day when Lilian was just about six months old, Henry decided to take her down to the docks of Crown Port, their hometown, to show her the ships, the open waters and maybe introduce her to a few of his sailing companions.

The shore was a few minutes stroll from the Finch household. During their walk, Lilian began to relax and nod off in the loving arms of her father. She put her tiny head down on her father's shoulder and breathed softly on his neck. He could tell she was just about asleep.

As they approached the waterfront, the smell of the salt air gripped Henry's nostrils and brought about that familiar longing to hit the open water. As he drew in a huge breath of ocean air, he felt little Lily stir in his arms. When they got closer to the water, Lily pulled her head up off her father's shoulder and turned her eyes to look directly at the horizon.

Henry couldn't believe the strength and focus Lily seemed to have while looking at the ocean. It was almost as if she knew what was out there and was drawn to it just as her father was. Suddenly, as they stepped onto the dock, Lily picked up her tiny arm, made a fist with her tiny hand, and then pointed, without a doubt, at the large sailing ship tied to the end of the dock.

"Yes, Lily, that's a sailing ship," he said, giggling with a sense of fatherly pride. "Do you like the ship, little girl?"

The two continued on until they reached the ship and heard a familiar voice calling out to them.

"Finch! Why Finch ye old Scallywag! Where've ye been?" It was Henry's longtime sailing buddy William Black, a fellow pirate and crew mate. "And by the light of the stars, this must be the little fellow I've heard tell of."

Lilian paid little attention to Black, and would not tear her gaze away from the ship, the water and that horizon. She was making all sorts of cooing noises, bubbly sounds and tiny baby giggles. She was enthralled by the sight of the sea.

"Well, Finch, looks like you may have a sailor on your hands," Black said, watching the baby's amazement boiling over. "Have you considered bringing him aboard as of yet?"

Henry tightened his hold on Lilian, coddling her head closer to the safety of his strong shoulders.

"No, no, not at all. Eventually, if he wants to take a voyage, we can discuss it. But as of now, the baby is just too young for our adventures," he said, being careful to use the word "he" as much as possible. "Maybe one day, he will want to venture out to that horizon. Until then, I'll be content to watch him grow."

Black looked at Henry with disbelief.

"You expect me to believe you will stay on land for more than a year's time? I don't believe it. That little one will be out here in no time. Mark my words, Finch. You won't be able to stay off the sea," Black stated matter-of-factly.

"I don't know, Black. Let's just give it some time for now," Henry said shortly, trying to change the subject. "So, where's the crew headed next?"

"We've not got a heading as of yet," Black said, rolling his eyes. "You know how the captain can be. Secretive he calls it. I call it ignorance on his part."

Henry laughed at his friend.

"You should be careful what you say, lad. Don't want to try out that plank, do ye, now?"

Black also began to laugh and the two shared a light moment of laughter together - something Henry hadn't done very often since he lost his wife, Lilian.

"Well," Black said, "I still say you have a sailor there. Just look at his gaze. Look into his eyes. It's there Henry. The same spark ye have when looking out to sea. I think he feels the pull already, at his young age."

"Be that as it may, Black. We'll not be heading out on any sailing adventures any time soon," Henry said. "But when we're ready, you'll be the first to know."

"I'll wait for the word, Finch. I'll wait for that little scabby to find his sea legs and then there will be no stopping you Finch boys. That I'm sure of."

Chapter 4

Henry "Dead Eye" Finch had been off the waters for six months and his stash of funds was slowly dwindling. From raising his daughter and surviving himself, he was running short on the money he had come by during his days at sea. Because his daughter was so young, he knew it was not yet the time to go back to his previous employment. This could mean only one thing. Finch would have to get a job; a land-lubber's job.

He decided he would start looking for employment right away.

Finch wrapped Lilian in a soft, white blanket and grabbed her favorite rag doll from her crib. The two of them left their home to solicit the town in search of a means of keeping their heads above water; for the time being, of course.

As father and daughter headed to town, Finch was naturally drawn to the docks. Out on one of the longer docks, he saw a group of men loading barrels and wooden boxes onto a large sailing ship.

"Those men are working for the dock, I'll just bet ye," he spoke to his tiny daughter who didn't understand the words, but enjoyed hearing her father's voice, and responded to the sound. "Do ye think I should approach them about work, Lily?"

The baby, as if she indeed *did* understand her father, squeaked in a way that said, "Yes, Daddy. I do think you should ask those men about work."

"Well, then it is so. Now, don't you make a poor showing. We want to get hired right away, darling," he said, giggling and straightening his hair a bit.

Finch approached the men who were working hard to load the barrels and heavy boxes into the cargo area of the giant ship. The men didn't seem to notice the man holding a small baby wrapped in a fuzzy blanket.

"Pardon me," Finch said.

No response.

"Please, I was wondering," Finch was cut off abruptly.

"Can't you see we're working here, sir," one of the men replied sternly. "We're on a time line and can't stop to chat whenever a visitor sees fit. We're shorthanded already!"

Perfect! Shorthanded, the man had said. That was very good news for Finch.

"I was just going to see about obtaining a job with you men and was inquiring of who I should speak with?"

The man who had responded suddenly stopped grabbing barrels and stood up, looking at Finch and his bundle.

"Would you like work for you *and* the babe?"

The other men looked up and began to snicker amongst themselves.

"Oh, no. Not the baby. Only for myself," Finch replied.

As if hearing the punch line of a joke, this sent the men into a fit of boisterous laughter.

"I'm sorry sir," the man said finally. "My men and I tend to get a bit unruly working out here in this blazing sun. Our manager is inside that office just there," the man said, pointing to a small shed-like building just off the dock. "You can speak with him if you wish."

"Thank you, sir," Finch said graciously. "Thank you so much."

Dead Eye and his daughter retreated from the dock-hands and headed for the office on land. He hoped this trip would be a cut and dry expedition, and he would leave the office with orders to return the following morning for work.

Dead Eye knocked on the wooden door marked "Silver Coin Loading Co." and almost immediately heard a rough voice tell him to, "Come on in!"

The voice sounded friendly and welcoming, so he opened the door and entered with a hopeful smile on his face.

"Hello good sir," said a small, round man sitting behind a wooden desk. "And who is this package of joy?"

"Hello. This is my...son," Dead Eye stammered for a second.

"And what a strapping young lad, I must say," said the round man. "And what can I do for you boys today?"

Finch cleared his throat and glanced down at the floor briefly.

"I was wondering if you had any positions available for work on the docks," Finch said to the man. "Ye see, my wife died in childbirth so it's just me and the little one. I was a sailor, but am land locked to take care of my son."

"Oh, I'm so sorry to hear about your wife, bless you both," said the man behind the desk. "I do need some more help out there, but what will you do with your young'un while you work?"

Dead Eye hadn't even thought of what would become of Lily when he went off to work. What would he do with Lilian while he worked? The baby couldn't stay home alone. And she couldn't come to the work place along with him. The only option would be to hire a nanny.

"I would hire a nanny, sir," Dead Eye finally replied. "I wouldn't bring the baby to work."

"Well, I should hope not!" the man said. "The docks are no place for a little one!"

The man looked down at some papers on his desktop. He shuffled through some things, and glanced at a chart on the wall behind him.

"Yes, yes I think we could use you, sir," the man said to Dead Eye. "When could you begin?"

"Oh, tomorrow sir," Dead Eye said with excitement. "As long as I can find someone to watch little Finch, I could be here tomorrow morning."

"Wonderful! Then I will see you at seven in the morning, all rested up and ready to work!"

"Thank you, sir, thank you," Dead Eye said. "By the way, the name's Finch. Henry Finch. And thank you again!"

Dead Eye and Lilian left the dock office with a victorious air. Now all Dead Eye needed to do was hire a nanny. But where would he look? Where do the ladies gather? He thought for a moment, and then remembered when his wife Lilian was still alive, there was one place she would always meet her lady friends. That place was the small café downtown. That place was Estelle's Bakery. And that was where he was headed next.

Chapter 5

s Henry and Lilian approached the quaint sweet shop, he straightened his hair again, and made sure his shirt was still tucked nicely into his trousers. He pulled open the door and was faced with a sea of wide, doe eyes and flowing gowns. The ladies were definitely all here.

"Henry!" one of the women greeted the pair as they entered.

Dead Eye couldn't make out which lady had called his name until a tall, thin, dark haired woman stood up in the far corner and started toward him. It was Gabrielle Locke, one of his wife's best lady friends. Henry smiled and walked to meet her.

"Hello, Henry, and hello, little one! My, the baby is growing so quickly. How time passes. How are you Henry?" This last question was spoken with deep sympathy and care. Gabrielle had been very close to Lilian, and obviously shared his sadness.

"We're doing alright, considering," Henry told Gabrielle, as Lilian picked up her head to look in the direction of the new voice. "Actually, I just got a job at the docks to help out with finances, and came here hoping to find someone who wouldn't mind watching a little one while his daddy goes off to make a living."

"Henry, I would be honored to watch the baby! It would make me feel so much closer to Lilian to take care of the greatest gift she ever gave to you," Gabrielle said sincerely. "When do you need me?"

Henry considered Gabrielle's offer, and decided one of Lilian's best friends would be a perfect choice to watch Finch.

"Well, I start tomorrow at seven in the morning," Henry said. "And I can pay you for your help after I receive my first pay."

"Then I'll be at your house at six-forty-five, and I don't expect any pay, Henry. I'm doing this for my friend Lilian."

"But," Henry started.

"No buts Henry," Gabrielle insisted. "I would feel devilish taking pay for something I would be so happy to do."

"Thank you Gabrielle, thank you. You've no idea what this means to me," Henry said, choking back tears of joy. "If you'd like, you can come by later, and I'll show you everything you need to know to deal with this little fella."

"I'll be over after dinner then," Gabrielle said with enthusiasm. "See you then, Henry Finch!"

Gabrielle headed back to her table, and Henry turned and went back out of the small, lady-filled café. Suddenly, a terrifying thought struck Henry. If Gabrielle was going to watch over Lilian, that would mean she would be tending to the baby's bathroom issues. There was no possible way to hide Lilian's femininity from her care taker.

Henry would explain the entire situation to Gabrielle when she arrived. Hopefully, she would understand and not think ill of him.

For now, it was time to get back to the Finch household and prepare for the following day. Many things were about to change, but Dead Eye felt everything was falling into place. The future was definitely looking brighter.

Gabrielle sat holding little Lilian while Henry explained why he had identified her as a boy since she was born.

"I can't say that I absolutely approve, but I do understand," Gabrielle said, smoothing Lilian's hair down on her tiny head.

"And you'll keep our secret then?"

"Of course I will. This little one deserves to be with her daddy, even if it involves a white lie," Gabrielle told Henry approvingly.

So from that day forth, Gabrielle took care of baby Lilian while Henry earned the family money until the time when the two could cast off to sea together.

Chapter 6

"Daa!"

Henry Finch heard his daughter's voice ringing out through their small, but cozy home in Crown Port.

"Daa!!"

"What is it child? What's the yelling all about?"

As Henry rounded the corner and stepped into two-year-old Lily's tiny bedroom, he saw what caused the hollering. Lily had found a small, wooden box, a small piece of fabric and several pieces of string. With these few items, she had managed to create the likeness of a large, sailing ship - a pirate ship.

"Why, what have you made you little genius?"

The toddler reached down and picked up her creation. She handed it to her father with a look of pride and accomplishment on her chubby, rosy-cheeked face.

"This is amazing, Lily. How...," he trailed off as he turned the ship around and around in his hands, marveling at the creativity of his young daughter.

"To me, Daa. Pweeze?" Lily said, holding her tiny hands up to her father, hoping to have the toy ship back in her possession.

"Of course, darling," her father said. "Here ye go."

He noticed the careful way she took and held her creation. She was growing into an interesting, young girl. He just wished everyday could be like the weekend when he didn't have to leave the girl and work on the docks. Time away from Lilian was difficult, but he knew he had to keep bringing home money to ensure a truly lovely childhood for his daughter.

Henry left the child alone to play with her ship in an imaginary world where only she knew of the adventures and excitement that lay waiting. As he rounded the corner leaving her bedroom, he heard her babbling and laughing in play. In the midst of the baby talk, Henry could have sworn he heard her say, "Ahoy crew!" as if greeting her shipmates prior to a long voyage out at sea. He stopped for a brief moment, listened again, then shook his head in amazement and continued on his way.

She was growing into an interesting young girl, indeed.

Chapter 7

Lilian continued to grow into a fine young lady.

She visited the docks often with her father and became familiar with the people and social scene associated with the life of a sailor.

Even though she never actually *questioned* her father, Lilian, who was now six years old, began to wonder why her hair wasn't long and beautiful like the other girls. She also started to notice that her clothes were different from the skirts and fancy blouses that the other little girls wore to church on Sunday.

Her father sensed that the young girl was beginning to see herself as different from the other children. He knew the time had come to have a talk with Lilian and explain everything.

"Lilian, could you come in here for a moment?" Henry called to his daughter from the sitting room. She was in her bedroom drawing a picture of a young girl hunting for treasure. The girl had long flowing hair and was wearing a frilly skirt that hung down to her shiny shoes. It was a very detailed drawing.

"Yes, Father?"

"Come in and sit with me for a while child. There are some things I want to talk to ye about."

Henry was sitting in his favorite chair in front of an open window. There was a slight breeze drifting in from the direction of the sea. Lily approached him and plopped onto the floor at his feet. She was holding the drawing in her hand.

"I want to talk to you about some things also, Father," Lilian said, matter-of-factly. She pointed to the young girl in her drawing.

"Why don't I look like her?"

Henry looked at the picture, and then looked at his daughter.

"What do you mean, Lily?" he asked, already knowing what she was referring to.

"She has long, pretty hair and mine is short like yours. And her clothes are fancy and lacy, but I wear trousers and a shirt like the men wear. Why, Daddy?"

Henry drew in a deep breath and leaned forward in his chair so he could get closer to his lovely daughter.

"Lilian, when you were on your way to this world, your mother and I were so happy. We had so many plans and dreams for our family. But when we lost your mother, many things changed.

"Do you know how I always made my living?" he asked Lilian.

"You're a sailor, Daddy," she said with a big smile.

"That's right, Lily. Do you know what kind of sailor I am?"

Lily looked puzzled. She knew her father sailed on big ships in the ocean. She had listened to stories of his adventures all her life. She also knew her father was very loyal to his captain and crew. She thought hard for a minute.

"Daddy, are you a pirate?"

Once again, Lilian Finch had stunned her father with an intelligence that went far beyond her years.

"Lily, how did you know that?"

She shrugged her shoulders nonchalantly and handed her drawing up for her father to take from her.

"The girl in the picture is me and she is searching for treasure," she said sternly. "She's searching for pirate's treasure."

Henry stared at his daughter's picture. Nothing in the drawing indicated that the girl was a pirate, or that she was searching for pirate treasure. However, that's exactly what his daughter had drawn.

"You're correct Lily. I am a pirate. I've been a pirate since I was born. I sailed my first voyage with my father when I was nine years old and was out to sea most of my life after that first trip. That is, up until about nine years ago when I met your mother here in Crown Port."

Lily put her hand up and looked as if she wanted to say something. She was silent for a moment, then asked a question Henry knew would come.

"Daddy, some pirates hurt people. Some just look for treasure and new ships and things to sell. Did you ever hurt anyone?"

Henry had indeed swindled his share of sailing ships and seized many another man's loot, but he had never killed or badly injured another human. He was proud of that.

"Never very badly," he said. "I've been in a few brawls and maybe thrown a few punches, but no, Lily, I've never killed anyone nor have I hurt anyone badly."

"That's good," she said. "So what happened nine years ago when you met my mother? Why did you stop sailing?"

"Well, the crew and I had docked here in Crown Port for a short stay and were visiting The Mermaid Tavern when I saw her standing behind the bar washing mugs. She was the prettiest lady I had ever laid eyes on."

"What did you do, daddy? Did you talk to Mommy?" Lilian asked, now totally intrigued and squatting up on her knees with growing excitement for this new story.

"Not right away, child. I didn't want to seem unruly or crass, so I waited until just the right moment," he continued.

"The next afternoon, I went down to The Mermaid alone, hoping to see the lady at work once again. Lucky for me, there she was a'sittin outside the tavern mending some aprons in the heat of the mid-day sun. She looked just like an angel."

He paused for a moment imagining how his wife had looked on that day. It was still difficult for him to believe she was gone.

"What then, Daddy? Did you go to her then?" Lilian broke the silence with her excited questions.

"Yes, Lily I did. I cleared my throat, straightened my hat, walked over to the beautiful creature and froze."

"You froze?" she asked in surprise.

"I froze up solid. Couldn't talk or move or even make a silly sound!" he said.

"Oh, no! What did she do?"

"Well, your mother looked up at me because I had stepped directly into the sunlight and thrown a shadow on her whole operation. She saw me silently looking down at her, and finally she said, 'Good day, sir.' That was it. With that one simple greeting, all my nerves relaxed and I thawed out completely. I greeted her in return, and we struck up a conversation that would rival some of the best exchanges between those who had known each other forever. It wasn't but a few months and she had agreed to take my hand in marriage."

"What a lovely story! You must have been so happy," Lilian said, now sitting up on her knees with her head resting on her hands over the arm of her father's chair.

"I was very happy Lily, except for one thing. I didn't want to leave your mother here alone, so I didn't go on as many sailing adventures as I had in the past. But I was alright with the situation, and the captain said I could sail with them anytime I wanted.

"So your mother and I bought this little home and made our settlement here in Crown Port."

"That's a great story, Daddy. Thank you so much for telling me," Lilian said, standing up straight in front of her father. "Now I have a question about something else."

"Go right ahead and ask, young lady."

"When may I go on a voyage with you, as you did with your father?"

Henry "Dead Eye" Finch sat back in his chair and breathed a long, heavy sigh.

Henry told Lily he would love to have her go sailing with him, and that was one reason he had always cut her hair short and dressed her in boys' clothes.

"So everyone really thinks I'm a boy?" she questioned.

"Yes Lilian. It's because pirates, and sailors alike, believe it to be bad luck to have a female on board their ship. When your mother passed on, I knew one day you would want to go to sea with me, but I also knew if the captain and crew knew you as a little girl, they would never agree to have you sail along.

"I decided right away to disguise your feminine qualities while in public so that when this day finally came, there would be no question of whether you could sail or not.

"I'm sorry for keeping all of this from you. But I can tell you are old enough to see you are a bit different from the other little girls."

They both sat quietly for a while.

Lilian was silently going over everything she had just heard. Henry was watching her face, trying to read her emotions.

Finally, Lilian looked up at her father, brushed back her short hair and smiled.

"I understand Daddy," she said clearly.

"Ye do? Are ye sure?" he asked in surprise.

"Yes. I'm glad you did something that would mean I would be able to stay by your side no matter what."

Henry had never thought of it all in quite that way, but as soon as the words escaped the babe's mouth, he knew that was exactly the reason he had made the decisions he had. He hadn't made everyone think his daughter was a boy only so she would be allowed on board the ship, but to protect their relationship. He did it to keep them together in a world where it may have been nearly impossible.

Chapter 8

Little Lilian Finch, at the fair age of 7 years old, had happened upon her father's sword. She instantly took a liking to the shiny, slim, slice of metallic beauty and, of course, wanted to play with it on her own terms.

When her father saw that she had discovered the weapon, he immediately ran to her and ripped her new-found toy from her hands.

"No Lilian! You mustn't play with such things! You could cut yourself or worse!"

Not understanding the severity in her father's voice, Lily pushed out her bottom lip, dipped her chin toward the floor and began to sniffle.

"But I just wanted to see it. I wasn't going to hurt myself, Daddy."

She kept her chin down, pushed the lip back out and raised her deep blue eyes to see if her father had been struck by her spell of innocence.

He had not fallen for her ploy. However, he decided if the girl wanted to investigate the cutlass, he would indeed teach her how to use it properly. After all, a bit of swordsman – or woman – ship may come in handy for Lilian someday.

"Stand firm, left foot out in front bearing your weight. Raise the cutlass higher. You want to appear ferocious and ready," Henry said, while demonstrating with another sword in his own hands.

"Now, as your opponent moves, you counter the movement by going the opposite direction," Henry said, demonstrating a keen, side-stepping motion. Lilian, as if by a natural grace born into her, countered his motion, brought the cutlass around and down, swooped her weapon upward and disarmed her stunned father.

A metallic clang rang out as his sword hit the floor at their feet. He looked at her in stunned silence for a moment.

"Lilian! That was incredible! How did ye learn such technique, such skill?"

"From you, Daddy," she said simply and went about holding the sword with a knowledge and strength not typical to such a young girl.

Henry watched the girl in a state of awe. She was a natural and was eager to learn. He decided maybe it was time to introduce her to his previous way of life, the time before she had come along. Henry believed Lilian was almost ready for her maiden voyage.

Chapter 9

"Happy Birthday to you,
Happy Birthday to you,
Happy Birthday dear little Finch,
Happy Birthday to you!"

Lilian puffed out her cheeks and blew as hard as she could to extinguish the 8 candles burning on her 3-tier birthday cake.

Some children from her neighborhood, Gabrielle and a few of her father's friends from the ship and the docks had gathered to celebrate her eighth birthday.

"Thank you all so much!" Lilian told her guests. "Father, could you help cut the cake?"

"Sure thing, Finch," her father said, grabbing the knife from the table. "Finch gets the first slice!"

Henry cut the cake and distributed a piece of the birthday treat to each of the guests. It was so delicious, Lilian asked for a second slice.

After everyone had finished their cake, the children went to play in the yard, while Gabrielle cleaned up and the men sat around a fire talking and drinking ale from large, pewter mugs.

The air was light and breezy. Lilian thought it may be the best day of her life.

Suddenly, Henry stood and, in a loud voice, asked for everyone's attention. Lilian had no idea what her father was about to announce.

"As you all know, my son has just turned eight years old," he paused as the crowd cheered for Lilian. "Therefore, I, Henry Dead Eye Finch will soon be accompanying young Finch on his maiden voyage aboard the Blue Mist!"

A loud cheer went up from the crowd.

"Ahoy mate!" someone shouted.

"Aye scallywag!" another guest hollered.

Lilian ran to her father and threw her arms around him. He hugged her back and lifted her high into the air.

"Oh, thank you Father!" she exclaimed. "Are you sure I'm ready for the sea?"

"Of course ye are Finch!" he smiled. "Ye were born ready."

"Thank you so much! When do we leave?"

Everyone laughed at Lilian's enthusiasm.

"Soon, Finch, soon," Henry told his daughter. "There are some loose ends that need tying up here on land before we head out to sea."

Lilian found it difficult to fall asleep that night after celebrating her birthday and hearing the news of her upcoming maiden voyage. Finally, she found herself drifting off into a restless, but welcomed sleep. She knew her night would be filled with sweet dreams of the open waters and high sea adventures.

When Henry Finch arrived for work the following day, he informed his boss that he would be leaving his position on the docks to head back out to sea. His child was old enough to accompany him on the ship, and he had decided it was time to set sail once again.

Lilian's nanny Gabrielle had taken wonderful care of the child, and was sorry to see Finch and Henry leave the shores, but she had always known the day would come.

"Take care out there," Gabrielle said to Lilian. "I know you can survive those waters, just try to keep those men in line, would ye?"

Lilian giggled and hugged her nanny tightly.

"I'll miss ye, Gabby," Lilian said. "We'll visit soon."

"My prayers will be with you and your father, Lily. Now, go. Explore the world! Just be sure to eat correctly and get the proper amount of sleep to keep ye well."

"I will Gabby, I will," Lilian said.

Chapter 10

Lilian had just turned 8 years old, and could not wait to board the ship – the Blue Mist - with her father. William Black, Sam Smythe, Captain Wellington and the entire crew were excited to welcome back their brother Dead Eye and his strapping young boy, Finch.

Lilian pulled on her tough, black trousers. She layered a soft, white camisole under a long-sleeved, button-up, stiff sailor-style top and red vest. She tied a square of black fabric over and around her head, hiding her short, but curly brown hair which did appear quite feminine despite the length. She sat down on the floor and yanked her high black boots over her dainty feet and up her calves.

Once she had the boots just right, she jumped to her feet, grabbed her belt and buckled it loosely around her tiny waist. The finishing touch was her father's sword. Lily slid the scabbard containing the weapon onto her belt. She took a deep breath and looked herself over once more. Feeling ready, she turned to her bedroom door and was about to open it when a sharp knock came from the other side.

"Yes?" she said, startled.

"Are ye ready, sailor?" her father asked.

She threw open the door and put her hands high in the air.

"How do I look, Daddy?" she asked, looking like a seasoned seaman.

Henry looked at his daughter with pure love and adoration. He couldn't believe they were about to take to the sea together. It seemed like just yesterday he held her in his arms for the first time. That day, so long ago, when he had been given the gift of a daughter, but had been deprived the companionship of his loving wife. Thinking of his wife made him realize how much Lilian was beginning to look like her mother. The resemblance was uncanny. Even disguised as a male, Lilian was just as beautiful as her late mother.

"You look wonderful, Lily – I mean, Finch, my son," he said with a wink. "Let's go, sailor."

Hand in hand, Henry "Dead Eye" Finch and his daughter, disguised as a boy, left their cozy home to set out on the adventure of a lifetime.

Chapter 11

"Secure the riggin'!"
"Unfurl that sail!"
"Prepare to hoist anchor, ye scurvy dogs!"

Capt. James Wellington bellowed orders to his crew. Despite the whipping wind and crashing surf, Wellington's voice boomed over the churning sea. The beginnings of a storm were brewing and Capt. Wellington hoped to be well out to sea before the worst of the squall hit Crown Port.

Henry and Lilian rounded the corner and were face to bow with the ship that would be carrying them across the ocean for young Lilian's maiden voyage.

"There she is Lilian. Are you ready to board?" Henry asked his daughter.

"Yes sir. I mean, aye sir!" Lilian said in a slightly lower voice. "That's my boy voice, alright Father?"

"Yes, yes Finch. That will do just fine. Now, let's join our crew."

Henry and Lilian began their ascent up the gang plank to the main deck of the Blue Mist. Men were bustling all around the deck preparing for their departure.

"Finch!"

It was William Black.

"So, this is the big day, eh? Little Mr. Finch's maiden voyage. So, lad, are ye ready for some adventure?" Black asked and slapped the young girl on her shoulder. She flinched a little, and then straightened up quickly.

"Aye, sir. I've been ready since I was young, sir," Lilian said.

The men giggled at the 8-year-old. She was very grown up, indeed.

"Ahoy! Come on now, let's get set to sail!" crew member and legendary pirate Francis Morgan called to the Finch men.

"Good to see you Dead Eye. And this must be your boy. Welcome aboard, young one. What do they call you lad?"

Lilian glanced at her father. He stuttered a bit, and then told Morgan to just call the boy Finch.

"Finch will do until he earns his sea name, that is," Dead Eye said with forced enthusiasm.

He realized he would need to work hard to break his habit of referring to his daughter by her real, birth-given name, Lilian. After all, she had been Lilian to him for eight years. He just prayed that he wouldn't slip.

"Wind in the sails, men!" called Capt. Wellington. "Fare thee well, Crown Port!"

"Argghhh!!" An excited cry went up from the entire crew and the Blue Mist finally left its dock heading for the open seas.

"Come Finch. We need to claim a bunk and secure our belongings below," Henry said to his daughter.

Their voyage was about to begin and Dead Eye knew for sure that it was going to be an adventure neither of them would ever forget.

Chapter 12

The Blue Mist passed directly under the on-coming storm while heading out to the open ocean, leaving the cozy waters of Crown Port.

Dead Eye and little Finch found two bunks side by side just to the right of the wooden stairs that led below deck. The two crew members put their trunks down next to their wobbly beds and pulled out their blankets. Lilian began to spruce up her area when she noticed her father watching her work.

"A young sailing boy shouldn't be so neat, Finch," Dead Eye said with a slightly stern look.

"Oh, right." Lilian glanced at her neatly folded bed clothes, then back at her father.

She cautiously reached down and messed up her blanket. She looked up at her father again, and saw that he was struggling to hold back his laughter.

She stared at him for a moment, and then they both broke into uncontrolled laughter. Lilian grabbed her blanket, flipped it up into the air and let it fall down onto the bunk, crooked and willy-nilly.

"I have some things to get used to, don't I father?" she laughed.

"Yes, I'd say you do, *son*!

They both fell onto her wrinkled blanket, across her wobbly bunk and laughed together until tears of happiness streamed down their faces.

Chapter 13

Lilian Finch, the little girl dressed in boys clothing, stood leaning against the wooden rail on the starboard side of the Blue Mist's main deck.

The sun bounced off the sea turning each ripple into a wave of sparkling diamonds. From her eyes all the way to the horizon, the water glimmered in the brightness of the day. She felt as if she could stare at the vast openness for a million years.

"Finch! Young Finch! Avast?"

It was a burly pirate named Gruff. His name obviously came from his harsh voice.

"Um, I was watching out over the starboard side, sir," Lilian stammered.

The pirate continued to glare at her until she felt like jumping over the railing and swimming away.

Suddenly, the man boomed boisterously, "Well, get over here and help us raise this sail, young 'un!"

Startled, yet relieved, Lilian ran across the deck to a small mast and grabbed hold of one of the ropes used to raise the huge square of heavy material.

"Grab hold, son, and keep 'er steady," Gruff told Finch. "When the wind catches hold, it'll pull ye."

Finch held steady. Some of the other men had wrapped the rope around their arms in order to hold on even tighter. Lilian took her right hand and wrapped the scratchy rope around the wrist of her left arm. Then she twirled the rope around her right wrist and held it tightly in her grip. Next, she waited. Gruff pulled another rope and she watched as the huge, white sail began to rise. It rose, and rose and uncurled and unraveled until finally a gust of wind blew up and filled the sail with forceful, powerful air.

"Tie 'er off, men. Keep 'er sailin'," Gruff growled over the roar of the wind in the sail.

Finch took the rope off her arms revealing bright, red rashes where the rope had torn at her delicate skin. As she was rubbing the painful rope burns on her right wrist with her left hand, and still holding strong to the rope with her right hand, she felt someone tap her on the shoulder.

She turned and saw a young boy, maybe two or three years older than herself. He reached out to take the rope from her and she handed it to him without thinking. He smiled, she smiled and the boy tied up Lilian's rope, before walking away to assist with another rope.

Lilian looked up at the now fully open sail and felt the ship being moved across the water by the powerful wind. The feeling made her stomach drop and shiver. She could feel the excitement from her fingertips to her toes. At that moment, watching the sail wave in the salty ocean air, Lilian Finch knew she was exactly where she belonged. Lilian Finch, the pirate, belonged to the open sea.

"I'm ready, horizon," Lilian said aloud. "Bring on the adventure."

Book 2

Kidnapped!

Chapter 1

"My name's Billy."

Lilian tore her gaze away from the gigantic sail and looked at the young boy who had tied up her rope. He had his right hand extended in Lilian's direction.

"Hi!" the boy spoke again.

Lilian grabbed the boy's hand with her own right hand and shook it - hard.

"Whoa there, little guy," Billy said laughing. "That's some grip ye got there!"

Lilian stopped shaking Billy's hand and let it go.

"Sorry," she said sheepishly.

"It's okay," Billy said. "So, what's your name?"

"L....," Lilian stopped and stared bug-eyed at the boy. She had almost slipped and said Lilian! If she had made that mistake, her secret identity would have been blown, and everyone would know she was a girl. She had to keep the crew believing she was a boy or they would surely kick her and her father, Henry "Dead Eye" Finch, off the Blue Mist.

"L...et's see!" she said, pretending to play a game to masquerade her mistake. "Try to guess."

"Hmm," Billy pondered. "Is it Bobby?"

"No," she answered.

"Gus?" Billy asked.

"No way," Lilian said, wrinkling up her nose in disgust.

"Sammy?" he tried again.

"No, no, no!" she said beginning to grow impatient.

"I don't know, just tell me," Billy pleaded desperately.

"Okay, okay," Lilian gave in. "My father is Henry Dead Eye Finch, so everyone just calls me Finch. That is until I get my sea name, father says."

"Okay, then Finch. What should we do first?"

Lilian looked confused.

"First? What do you mean, first?"

"Well, we're the only two boys on this great, big ship. I suppose it's only natural that we should be friends and get into some mischief together!"

Lilian began to laugh, but suddenly realized Billy was being very serious.

"Oh, I don't know," she said. "My father wouldn't want me doing anything dangerous or against the rules of the captain."

"Argh, for the love of the sea, boy! This ship is full of pirates, including you and me. Do you really think there are rules against two kids having a little fun?" Billy said, trying to persuade his new friend.

Lilian paused and thought for a moment. She looked around at the pirates roaming the deck and working the ship. She supposed it was a fairly care-free place.

"Yes, I supposed you could be right, but..."

"Great!" Billy shouted. "Come on, lad. Let's go!"

Billy grabbed Lilian's arm and ran down the stairwell to the lower deck. It smelled musty down below, and grew darker and darker as they descended the steps.

When they reached the bottom of the staircase, they stopped. There were a few lanterns hanging from the walls, casting a dim light throughout the gloomy area.

"What is this place?" Lilian asked.

"It's the lower deck. We store stuff here and shoot the canons from here and down the other end is where your bunk is, barnacle brains! Come on!"

Billy took hold of Lilian's arm again and took off running, ducking and dodging through the boxes, barrels and piles of cannon balls which littered the damp, wooden floor of this new, adventurous place.

"Can we stop yet? You're pinching my arm!" Lilian said, yanking her arm out of Billy's strong grip.

"Oh. Sorry Finch. I got carried away. I'm usually stuck in this murky cavern by myself, so now that I have a partner to help on my mission, I'm very excited to get started."

"Mission? What's your mission?" Lilian asked cautiously.

"Treasure, of course!" Billy yelled, grabbing Lilian's shoulders and pulling her so close to himself that she felt his hot, stale breath on her face.

"Ugh!" she said and pushed him away. "Settle down! I get it! I get it!"

"I'm sorry, Finch. I didn't mean to..."

"It's alright mate," she said in her best boy voice. "I just wasn't ready for your rotten breath."

At that, Billy jerked his head up, ready to rebut her insult, when he noticed she was grinning. His embarrassment faded and he began to laugh.

"You're not like most boys I know, Finch," Billy said. "Something's different about you."

Lilian stopped and began to get nervous. *Oh no, she thought. He knows I'm a girl! He knows! I have to do something!*

So Lilian drew her right arm back, took a deep breath, and punched Billy square in the shoulder. Billy squealed and grabbed at his soon to be bruised arm.

"What was that for?" Billy asked Lilian who was trying not to nurse her own aching hand.

"I was just foolin' with ye, sailor," she said with a forced grin.

Billy rubbed his tender shoulder and smiled.

"Alright pirate. Let's find some treasure!"

Chapter 2

The two children began exploring the dark storage area in the under-belly of the Blue Mist.

Lilian was digging through an old abandoned trunk while Billy tried to pry open a locked storage closet under the stairs. He was using his dagger to wiggle the slot in the pad lock that was holding the door closed tight.

Lilian had come across a few interesting items in the trunk she was exploring; one of those being a small, but heavy hammer.

"Here, Billy. Give this a try," Lilian said, handing him the tool.

"Oh! That should work. Let's have it."

Billy took the hammer, held it high over his shoulder, eyed up his mark and swung hard at the lock.

"Ouch!" he cried, and dropped the hammer.

The impact of the heavy hammer on the strong, metal lock stung his hand.

Lilian giggled.

"Ye think ye can do better, then?" Billy said sarcastically.

"Sure, I'll give it a try. Give me the hammer," Lilian said, reaching out for the tool.

She took the hammer and lifted the lock up a bit to examine the place where the metal loop locked into the large, metal base. She thought if she hit the body of the lock at just the right spot, the lock's metal loop would let go.

She let the lock fall and rest against the closet door. She stepped over to the left of the closet door. She pulled the hammer back over her shoulder, aimed at the very spot she had chosen as the magic point on the lock and swung hard.

"Whoa!" Billy cheered as the lock popped open. "That was brilliant, lad!"

Lilian gazed at the open lock in amazement. She did it! She took a bow in acknowledgement of her accomplishment and tossed the hammer back into the trunk where she had found it.

"Well, you do the honors, Finch. You snapped the lock. Open the door!" Billy said excitedly.

"Alright," she said, swallowing nervously.

What might be in there? When was the last time this musty, old closet was even open? What if the contents of the closet were not very pleasant? What if...

"Come on Finch! I can't stand it!" Billy was nearly jumping up and down. "Open it!"

Lilian lifted the now open pad lock off the hook. Then she grabbed the door knob and pulled.

Cob webs spread between the door and its frame as the once closed space began to open and breathe again.

It was dark inside the closet, but the children could tell the space was full of mysterious objects.

"I'll grab a lantern," Billy said, running off to take a torch from a holder on the wall.

"Alright," Lilian said, still staring cautiously into the dark cavern.

Billy returned with the lantern and approached the open closet door. He shined the light cast by the flame into the dark closet.

Both Lilian and Billy stood frozen.

"Unbelievable," Billy finally said.

Lilian stood speechless.

Inside the closet were stacks and stacks of books. Thick books, thin picture books, books with brown covers and books with golden pages. There were more books in that closet than either of them had ever seen at one time.

"What is this? It looks like some kind of library," Billy asked.

"Well, there's enough books to fill one, but I don't think libraries are normally inside of a closet," Lilian responded, still in awe.

"I wonder where they all came from," Billy pondered.

"I don't know, but I love books and I'm going in," Lilian said, excited to dive into the newly found treasure.

"Wait!" Billy shouted at her. "Books are silly. That's not a treasure. That's just a lot of dusty, smelly junk. Let's go check out that trunk."

Lilian stared at Billy. She wasn't sure how to respond. She loved to read. Her father had started teaching her the alphabet and letter sounds when she was just a toddler and just beginning to talk. He helped her learn to read small books, and he read to her every night, pointing out words and phrases which she retained like a genius. She was a great reader and was proud of it.

"What do you mean, silly? Books are great!" Lilian said, peering into the closet trying to read some titles by the fire's glow.

"But you can't read," Billy stated. "You just look at the pictures, right?"

"Of course I can read," Lilian said nonchalantly.

She looked back at Billy and noticed the shameful look on his face. She immediately knew what was wrong. Billy couldn't read.

"I mean, I can read a bit, just the basic language, ye know," she said, trying not to make Billy feel bad. "My father taught me a little."

Billy's look changed from shameful to lofty.

"Well, you can waste your time with those frivolous things if you wish, but I'm going to go find something a bit more exciting to explore. I'll be over there," he said. He pointed to a broken down old trunk and walked away.

"I'm going to explore these books and find one to read. If you want to listen, that would be fine," she called after him.

Lilian warily entered the dank and dirty library closet. Soon she was surrounded by hills and mountains of books. She was swallowed up by hundreds of different worlds, people and stories.

"Now, this is going to be some adventure," she said, grabbing the first book she could reach.

Chapter 3

"Although the Soldiery retreated from the Field of Death, and encamped out of the City, the Contagion followed, and vanquish'd them; many in their Old Age, and others in their Prime, sunk under its cruelties."

Lilian began reading, <u>Loimologia</u>, aloud, to herself, seated in the middle of two large piles of books.

Billy sat absently by the mysterious trunk, all his attention on Lilian's voice spilling out of the open closet door. He couldn't help but listen to the fluent words escaping his friend's mouth.

"Of the Female Sex most died; and hardly any children escaped; and it was not uncommon to see an Inheritance pass successively to three or four Heirs in as many Days; the Number of Sextons were not sufficient to bury the Dead."

Soon Billy was seated just outside the closet door. She couldn't see him, but Lilian knew he was there. She closed that book, rooted through another stack of books and found a new one to dive into. The book she chose was entitled, <u>Mediation Upon a Broomstick</u>.

"But a Broom-stick, perhaps you'll say, is an Emblem of a Tree standing on its Head." She heard Billy giggle outside the

doorway. *"And pray what is Man, but a Topsy-turvy Creature, his Animal Faculties perpetually mounted on his Rational; His Head where his Heels should be; groveling on the Earth."*

Lilian paused. She sat quietly before beginning to read again.

"His last Days are spent in Slavery to Women, and generally the least deserving; 'till worn to the Stumps, like his Brother Bezom, he's either kicked out of Doors, or made use of to kindle Flames, for others to warm Themselves by."

"Amen!" Billy called out.

Lilian then heard what sounded like him slapping his hand over his loud mouth.

"Ha! I caught you!" she said, jumping out the door at her friend.

Billy was still covering his mouth in embarrassment.

"It's really alright Billy. Just come in and look through the books. We can read together," she said, hoping he would accept her invitation.

"Your father taught you well, Finch," Billy said admiringly.

"Thanks Billy," she said with a smile. "I'm a bit dry from all this reading aloud. Could we go find a drink in the galley?"

Lilian began to close the book she currently had open on her lap. Billy reached over quickly and put his hand inside the pages of the book.

"Sure we can," he said. "But don't lose your spot. I want to hear more of this one."

As the two friends were climbing the stairs to the main deck, they saw a hectic scene. Men were running about on the deck, looking from one side of the ship to the other. One pirate was high above them all, standing in the crow's nest with a long telescope to his eye.

"Land, ho!" he was yelling.

The crew members scurrying about the ship were preparing to make anchor off the coast of the island that was steadily growing larger on the horizon.

"Guess that drink will have to wait," Billy said, and he took off running to lend a hand with bringing the ship in safely.

Lilian stood by the wooden rail where she was out of the way, but could see all the action. As the ship drew closer to the island, tiny buildings began to emerge from the trees. She could see a dock stretching out into a harbor with several small fishing boats bobbing carelessly on the blue waters.

"Prepare to drop anchor, men!"

It was Capt. Wellington shouting commands to the crew.

Just then Lilian saw her father run to the huge wheel that held the anchor line.

"Father, can I help?"

"Of course you can! Get over here, mate!" he yelled with pride.

Happily, Lilian ran over to help her father and the other men anchor the Blue Mist in the waters of this mysterious, new port.

Chapter 4

With the Blue Mist securely anchored in the harbor, the crew lowered a few small row boats into the water and rowed to the dock. Lilian, along with her father, Billy and two other crew mates were the first to reach the dock.

The town they were about to explore was very small, but very inviting. There were fishermen, sailors, women and children all milling around casually on the long, wooden dock that extended out into the beautiful, green harbor. When Lilian's row boat pulled close to the dock, a friendly fisherman was waiting to greet them.

"Throw me a rope, lad," the fisherman shouted to Billy.

"Aye!" Billy replied. He picked up the prickly rope connected to the bow of the small boat and tossed it strongly to the stranger. The man on the dock caught it and pulled them over to the dock.

"Ahoy! And welcome to Emerald Harbor. Where ye hail from?" he asked, reaching down to help Lilian out of the row boat.

Her father spoke up from behind her. "Crown Port, sir," he answered.

"Ah, a lovely port of call, if I might say. Been there many a time me self," said the stranger.

After each member of the Blue Mist crew had climbed up onto the dock, the fisherman introduced himself as Charles Robins, a career fisherman who resides there in Emerald Harbor, but spends much time out on the sea making a living to support his wife and three young children.

"It's a tough life, but seeing the smiles on the faces of me kids makes everything worth the work," Robins said, with a proud grin of his own.

"I know just what ye mean, friend," Dead Eye said, putting an arm around his child's small shoulders.

"Ah, do we have a father and son sailing team here then?" Robins asked excitedly.

"Aye," said Dead Eye, looking at his daughter with a secretive smile.

"Well, then you'll want to be exploring our fine town, so I'll let you on your way," Robins said. "Be sure not to miss Mama Luella's Bakery. It be the best bakery in all the land."

"Thank you my friend. We'll head that way now. Starvin' we are," Dead Eye said, and they all bid Robins farewell.

"Father, if all the people here are as friendly as that fellow, we should have a great stay!" Lilian Finch said happily.

Unfortunately, they were about to discover that not everyone in Emerald Harbor was as friendly as Robins. Not even close.

Chapter 5

Dead Eye and his daughter Lilian wandered the seashell covered streets of Emerald Harbor taking in the sights and smelling the delicious smells.

"There be Mama Luella's," Dead Eye told his daughter, pointing to the cozy café.

Billy, Sam Smythe and Daniel Bonds were already seated along a bench outside the bakery.

"Finch!" Billy yelled to his friend. "Come eat! This is great!"

Lilian and her father entered the delightful smelling shop and gazed at the fresh baked goods that were laying on display along a sturdy, wooden counter.

" 'Ello friends, and welcome!" said an elderly woman from the back of the shop. "Can I get ye something for ye empty bellies?"

Lilian pointed to a large, spiral bun covered in cinnamon and sugar. "I'll take one of those," she said, her mouth watering.

"Make that two, please ma'am," Dead Eye said, ordering their food.

"Sure thing," Mama Luella said, handing them their goodies.

Dead Eye paid for the buns and escorted his daughter out the door to the bench where their crew mates had been sitting. However, when they reached the bench, it was empty. Just as they were wondering what happened to the three men, shouting drew their attention to the middle of the street.

Billy, Sam and Daniel were nose to nose with three salty-looking sailors. The unpleasant strangers were apparently not happy with the Blue Mist crew.

"Aye, and why have ye come to Emerald Harbor? What be your business with us?" asked one burly, dirty man.

"We have no business with you and you need not know why we've come here. It is none of your concern," Sam Smythe said bravely, pushing his chest out only to meet the stomach of the huge man.

"None of MY business is it? Listen here boy, I AM Emerald Harbor. You have come here without invite. You need to state your purpose or move on, if you know what's good for ye and your crew," the huge man said, grabbing Sam by the collar of his shirt and lifting him off the ground.

"Slow down now gentlemen. Let's talk this out and no one will get hurt," Dead Eye said, grabbing Sam from the stranger and moving him aside, out of harm's way.

Dead Eye put out his hand. "Hello fellows, I'm Henry Dead Eye Finch of Crown Port. We happened upon your harbor in our travels and have no specific business with you. I'm sorry if there's been a misunderstanding. No harm meant," Dead Eye finished and waited for the gigantic, bearded man to return his gesture in a hand shake.

"Bah!" the man shouted instead. "You'd be smart to move on sailor. "This be no place for a young crew like yours. Come."

The huge man turned, motioned to his crew and disappeared around the corner of the bakery.

"What was that all about?" Lilian asked Billy, taking a bite of her cinnamon bun.

"I don't rightly know, but we're going to find out. Come on!" Billy grabbed Lilian's left hand and headed for the corner where the unwelcoming gang had just disappeared. In the process, Lilian dropped the rest of her treat.

"Ugh, thanks a lot Billy," she groaned, and went on with her friend.

Dead Eye, Sam and Daniel were in a huddle in the middle of the street and didn't notice when the two youngsters ran off.

Billy peered around the corner.

"Do you see them?" Lilian asked.

"Aye!" Billy told her. "They just slipped into a backdoor down there. Come on!"

"I don't think..." Lilian was cut off when Billy jerked her arm again, pulling her down the alley way.

They reached the door where Billy had seen the men disappear, and put their ears near the door jamb, listening for voices.

"Arghh!!!"

They heard a loud cry go up from behind the door, followed by bellowing laughter.

Lilian and Billy looked at each other warily.

"Did ye see the scared faces of those intruders?" one boisterous townsman shouted between giggles. "Bly if they won't be runnin' for the sea by now!"

Billy jumped back from the door.

"How dare they laugh at our crew?" Billy shouted. "Who do they think they are?"

"Shhh!" Lilian said, pulling Billy down to squat by the door. "They'll hear you!"

Suddenly, they realized it was quiet on the other side of the door. The rusty, old door knob began to jiggle.

"Hide!" Billy yelled. But it was too late. The door swung open and a gigantic hand closed over the back of Billy's shirt collar.

The next moment, Billy was dangling high in the air by his shirt, feet swinging freely in the breeze.

"Aye, and what do we have here?" the huge, smelly man yelled loudly into Billy's face. "It looks like there's a spy in our midst, boys!"

Billy kicked, and struggled, and swung his fists at his captor in an effort to escape, but it was no use. He could not get away.

"Put him down!" Lilian jumped up and began pounding on the large man's back. Meanwhile, the rest of his crew came through the doorway and were having a laugh at the children's expense.

"Boys, is there a bug on me back? I keep feelin' tiny bites."

They all bellowed and howled with laughter. One of them finally grabbed Lilian around her shoulders and pulled her away from her target.

"What shall we do with these pests, boss?"

"Well, since they're so interested in what's going on behind this here door, let's give 'em a tour," the big man said, still holding Billy up in the air.

"Arghh!" shouted the unruly bunch.

They dragged the youngsters to the door and shoved them into a dark, damp room. Lilian looked at Billy.

Kidnapped!

"I think we're in trouble," she said, her voice quaking, as the big door slammed shut, trapping the children in the room with the frightening crew.

Chapter 6

"I understand Sam, but we've just arrived in this town, and we don't need any trouble," Dead Eye lectured Sam Smythe who had almost gotten into a scuffle with a gruff townsman.

"Besides, young Billy here...," Dead Eye trailed off as he turned to where Billy had been standing, and saw that he was gone. "Where is the lad?" he asked, concerned. Just then he realized Lilian was also missing.

"Where's Finch?" Dead Eye yelled. "Where are the children?"

The three men, Dead Eye, Sam and Daniel looked up and down the street. They looked inside the bakery and over on the bench.

"Where in heavens have they disappeared to?" Dead Eye wondered aloud.

"I may have an idea," Daniel said, pointing down the alley. "That's where those men went, and if I know Billy, he took Finch and followed them. Billy likes to be the hero."

"Let's hope not. Those fellows weren't the type to fool with," Sam said, as Dead Eye took off running down the alley.

Daniel and Sam turned to follow and heard Dead Eye yelling, "Finch! Billy!"

Dead Eye saw the closed door and thought nothing of it until he heard a thump come from the other side.

"What was that?" Sam asked, as he came running to join Dead Eye.

"It came from that door," Dead Eye said. "Try to open it."

Sam grabbed the rusty door knob and turned it clockwise. The knob turned, but the door didn't open. He figured there was a padlock on the other side of the door.

"Knock on it!" Daniel said.

Sam began to knock, but to no avail.

"Oh, move out of the way," Dead Eye said, shoving Daniel to the side. "Hello. Is there anyone there?"

He pounded hard on the door. Finally, a voice from the other side answered his plea.

"Aye, what do ye want?"

"Have you seen two young boys? They were with us, now they've gone and we need to find them."

"No boys," the voice replied unsympathetically.

Dead Eye's face fell.

"Are ye sure? They're just boys. About this tall, young," Dead Eye pleaded.

There was no response from the other side.

Dead Eye waited for an answer, growing more worried and angry by the second. He looked at Sam and Daniel. They both looked puzzled and worried.

"I know they're in there! I know those brutes took them and I'm not leaving without Lilian!!"

Sam and Daniel looked at each other, more puzzled than ever.

"Lilian?" Sam asked.

"I...I mean Finch. I slipped. I still miss my wife. I lost her and I'll not lose my...son," Dead Eye saved himself with a satisfactory correction.

"Now, I'm going in there with or without you two, and I'm going to find Finch and Billy."

Chapter 7

The big man who appeared to be the leader of the band of scallywags was called Dusty McCray. Lilian heard one of his minions address him as such after being belittled by the bully himself.

Lilian and Billy were seated on a damp, wooden bench. A creepy man who wheezed rather than breathed normally tied their hands and feet together so there was no chance of them escaping.

The room where they were being held had only one window which was covered with heavy cloth, only allowing a sliver of light on each side of the fabric to enter the room.

The children had no clue where they were and no idea if anyone was even looking for them.

"What are we going to do?" Lilian whispered to Billy. "I'm scared."

"Don't be scared, Finch. I'll get us out of this," Billy said confidently.

"Hush up over there you two, or I'll shut you up myself," said a gruff man who was assigned to keep an eye on the children.

Billy and Lilian exchanged worried glances. Then Billy silently told Lilian it was going to be okay, and motioned for her to look at the rope holding his hands together. He showed her that he was slowly working the rope loose, and would soon have his hands free.

Lilian followed her friend's lead and began to wiggle her hands and wrists in the hopes of loosening her ropes, too. The rope was scratchy and splintery and scraped her tender skin, but the discomfort didn't discourage her efforts.

Suddenly, Billy cleared his throat loudly to get her attention. He had gotten free! He put a finger to his lips, telling her to stay silent, then reached down and pulled the rope off his feet. Billy was free!

Quickly, before anyone could see what was happening, Billy finished loosening the ropes on Lilian's hands then freed her feet.

The man who was supposed to be watching them had drifted off into a nap. Being careful not to wake him, the two children snuck over to the lone window and moved the curtain aside.

"Blast!" Billy whispered with disappointment.

The window was covered on the outside with iron bars. Even though they were free of their ropes, the children were still trapped.

"What are we going to do now?" Lilian asked Billy. "We'll never get out this window!"

"No kidding, Finch," he said with some irritation. "So, we have to find another way out."

Billy looked around. The only other exit to the outside was the door they had been brought through. However, that door was pad locked, and there was no sign of a key. But what Billy did see was a hammer. He remembered how Finch had blasted the pad lock off the library closet with a hammer, and knew his friend could do it again here. Finch could set them both free.

Chapter 8

"Just swing hard, Finch and hurry!" Billy pleaded. "He could wake up any time!"

Lilian grasped the wooden handle of the heavy hammer with both of her hands. She took a deep breath and blew out hard. She inhaled again, lifted the tool above her head and swung.

Everything happened so quickly. They heard a loud crack, saw the lock tumble to the floor and felt the floor rumbling as the man ran after them.

"Hurry!" Billy said, grabbing Lilian's arm and darting through the now open door.

Billy ran right into something that felt like a brick wall.

"Finch! Billy! You've escaped!"

It was Henry "Dead Eye" Finch. The children were safe.

"Get back here ye grubby lads!" the huge man yelled.

"Come on, kids. Let's get you outta here," Dead Eye said, picking up one child in each arm and heading out of the alley and into the street.

As the big man attempted to run though the open doorway and out into the alley, he slammed his head on the top of the door frame and knocked himself flat.

Dead Eye turned just in time to see the man collapse onto the floor.

"Well, we don't have to worry about him anymore. Have a look," Dead Eye said with a giggle.

The kids turned and saw their captor unconscious on the floor, half inside and half outside the room that had been their prison.

"Dumb ol' lump head," Billy said.

Lilian laughed whole heartedly and turned to hug her father in relief.

"Okay you two. No more running off. No more heroes, got it?"

"Yes, sir," they said in unison.

"Very good, lads. Let's get back to the ship and back out to sea," Dead Eye said, leading the way to the dock.

Chapter 9

Lilian Finch and her new found friend Billy had survived their first adventure. No doubt the twosome would find themselves in many more exciting and precarious situations; maybe even sooner than expected.

But for now, the children were back on board the Blue Mist and Capt. Wellington was planning their next journey.

"Due South, gentlemen, to the lower Caribbean," Capt. Wellington announced.

Lilian had not yet visited the southern-most points of the Caribbean Sea and felt a pang of excitement upon hearing their new heading.

"I can't wait to see all the different fish and sea life, Father," Lilian said.

"Ye can see through all the way to the bottom of the sea," he said dreamily. "It's beautiful, Finch. I'm so happy we'll get to see it together."

"Me too, Father," Lilian said.

She hugged her father tightly then let go and walked over to the wooden rail. She peered into the blue-green water and could hardly imagine what was beneath the surface.

Lilian knew there were millions of beings living down there just out of her sight. But what exactly lived in those waters?

Suddenly, she knew what to do. Lilian descended the wooden stairs to the lower deck and went straight to the library. She spent the rest of the day looking through hundreds of books about sea life.

There were so many beautiful creatures that lived in the ocean. As she looked at the pictures, she couldn't believe she would soon see some of these fish with her own eyes.

"Aye," she said aloud to herself. "Bring on the Caribbean."

Book 3

Tragedy and Freedom

Chapter 1

Lilian Finch, now 11 years old, rolled over on her small bunk and slowly opened her eyes. The dark, damp under belly of the Blue Mist was extremely warm. They were sailing in the Caribbean Sea and the temperature outside was hot and steamy even at this early hour.

Lilian flipped back her thin blanket and sat up, swinging her bare legs over the edge of her cot.

"Good morning," a scratchy voice breathed from behind her.

"Good morning!" Lilian said, turning to glance at her father, Henry "Dead Eye" Finch, the pirate.

"What be your plans for today?" Dead Eye asked his daughter.

"Not sure yet," she answered. "Billy wants to go down to the library for a while, then maybe some deck ball later."

When they were younger, Lilian and her friend Billy discovered a large storage closet below decks. Inside the closet they found piles and piles of books.

Because Lilian was an outstanding reader and Billy had never learned, they spent much of their time in what they now called "their library" reading stories.

"That sounds like a fun day," Dead Eye responded. "Just be careful."

Dead Eye could see his daughter growing and knew the façade was getting more difficult for her.

He wasn't sure pretending to be a boy was the best thing for her anymore, but he did know she loved being out at sea and the only way for her to stay with him and the crew of the Blue Mist was to remain a boy. A boy named Finch.

Chapter 2

"There was no possibility of taking a walk that day. We had been wandering, indeed, in the leafless shrubbery an hour in the morning; but since dinner (Mrs. Reed, when there was no company, dined early) the cold winter wind had brought with it clouds so somber, and a rain so penetrating, that further out-door exercise was now out of the question."

"Brilliant, Billy!" Lilian exclaimed. "You are officially a great reader!"

"Thanks to you, Finch," he said gratefully. "If I hadn't met you, I might still be dumb."

"You were never dumb! Don't say such things," Finch scolded. "And I'm glad I could help. Now, what say we go up and play some deck ball?"

"Right!" Billy replied, and they headed up the stairs.

When they reached the main deck, they came face to face with a frantic, chaotic scene.

"Lower the main sail! Secure the riggin'!"

Capt. James Wellington commanded his crew to secure the ship for what appeared to be one heck of a squall.

The sky had turned a deep shade of purple which made the gray puffy storm clouds appear to pop right out of the solemn canvas.

The wind was blowing so hard, the children could barely keep their footing on deck.

"Finch! Billy!"

Dead Eye hollered to them from his post holding a rope near the wooden rail of the massive ship.

"Get back down below! Hurry! It's too dangerous up here!" he ordered them.

"But father, I want to help!" Lilian began.

"No Finch! The storm's too rough! I'll get ye when it's passed," he yelled over the roar of the wind. "Take care Finch. I love you, my child!"

"Come on," Billy said, taking Lilian's arm and guiding her back down the stairs.

"But we could help. I'm sure there's something we could do!" Lilian protested at the bottom of the wooden stairs.

"No, Finch. We need to stay here this time. We need to stay out of the way and out of trouble. The crew will handle it and retrieve us when they need us," Billy explained.

Chapter 3

Three years out to sea and Lilian had never experienced a storm such as the one that was currently attacking their ship.

She had never felt the ship rock and sway the way the Blue Mist was quaking now. She was scared. She was worried about the ship holding up against the storm's fury. But mostly, she was petrified for her father.

Dead Eye was up on the deck trying to help sail the ship through this monster squall. She had last seen him he was near the railing and that made her nervous.

Billy saw the worried look in his friend's eyes.

"Don't worry, Finch, you'll be fine," he told her, patting her on the back.

"It's not me I'm worried about. It's them," she said, pointing up toward the main deck.

"And your father," Billy replied, lowering his gaze away from her eyes.

"Yes," she answered.

"He's a brave and strong man. He'll be fine, Finch. He'll be down for us soon," he said.

Suddenly, the ship lurched to the right far enough to send both children tumbling across the floor.

The yelling from above – which had previously been drowned out by the storm – rose to a deafening roar.

"Something's wrong," Finch said, pulling herself up off the floor.

"No Finch! Don't!" Billy screamed, reaching for his friend who was now running for the stairs.

Billy was too slow getting up. Lilian ascended the stairs and was quickly up on the main deck.

"Finch! Finch!" one pirate was yelling over the side of the ship.

"Where is he, lads? Can ye see 'im?" another asked.

"Get a rope out there!"

"Hurry! There's no sign of him!"

The crew members were standing by the wooden railing, leaning over and looking into the churning sea. Someone had fallen overboard.

"Dead Eye!"

William Black, one of Dead Eye Finch's closest and dearest friends, was nearly climbing the wet, slippery railing, bellowing in desperation. With rain pelting his face, Black was yelling her father's name into the deep, blue sea.

"No!!" Lilian ran to the group of men by the rail and pushed her way to Black.

"Black! What happened?" she screamed, tugging on his trousers.

"Get Finch out of here, Sam," Black called to crew mate Sam Smythe.

"Finch, come on. There's nothing you can do here," Smythe said, grabbing her by the shoulders.

"No! Where's my father? Where is he?"

Finch was swinging her fists and screaming as Smythe led her to the stairs and back down to the lower deck.

Once out of the rain and in the quiet of the ship's under belly, Smythe fell to the floor and grabbed Lilian, pulling her close to him. Billy came closer, but gave them their space.

"Quiet now, child," he said soothingly. "Oh, great Lord above, why? Why twice for this fair babe?"

Smythe was holding Lilian, but seemed to be speaking to a higher power.

"Please, Sam, please," she pleaded. "Tell me what happened up there."

Smythe loosened his grip on Lilian and looked down into her eyes.

"My poor child, there's no easy way to tell ye. The sea took your father," he said, his voice breaking in grief. "He fell over the rail and the deep blue swallowed him whole."

Lilian stared at him in disbelief. Billy walked up behind her and put a hand on her shoulder.

"No," she sighed quietly. "No, he's fine. He'll climb back on board. He'll be fine."

Smythe held her close again, tears streaming from his eyes, down his cheeks and onto her head of short, cropped hair.

"I'm so sorry, lad," Smythe whispered.

Lilian pushed away from Smythe and stood so quickly it almost looked like one single motion. She looked at Billy who was standing wide eyed and stiff. She turned to run for the stairs, but suddenly her vision got blurry. Next, everything went black and she collapsed to the floor.

Chapter 4

"Finch? Finch, can you hear me?"

Lilian felt as if she was under the water. She felt groggy and heavy and she heard muffled voices in the distance.

"Come on Finch. Come back to me, friend."

She recognized the voice of her best friend Billy, but he sounded miles away.

"I don't know, Smythe. He's not even stirring," Billy said, with worry in his voice.

Lilian knew she had to fight to get back to her friend; to wake up.

She struggled to open her eyes. Finally, her eye lids lifted and the dim light poured in. She saw that William Black had joined them in the lower deck.

"There you are," Billy said, smiling at his friend.

"Dad," Lilian said hoarsely, trying to sit up.

"No, no you don't," William Black said to her, holding her down on the cot. "You took a wicked fall, lad. You stay put for a bit."

"But my dad, he," she trailed off as she remembered the tragedy that had unfolded during the terrible storm. She began to cry.

"There, there now. Let it out, Finch." Black carefully pulled her up by her shoulders and held her close to his chest.

"I'm so sorry, Finch," Billy said. "He was a great man. But we will all take care of you now."

Lilian continued to sob. How could this have happened? How could she be all alone in the world? Her mother had died while she was giving birth to her, and now her father had fallen victim to the sea which they had loved so much together.

She was alone; an orphan with nothing but her secret.

"Billy, could you go and get Finch some rum to calm him down," Black asked.

"But he's only a child," Billy began.

"I know that, but he's man enough to have a drink to settle his nerves. Now go."

Billy went off to fetch a drink for Lilian who was sobbing fiercely in Black's arms.

"Your father was like a brother to me," Black said. "I want you to remember him as the brave, courageous man...pirate that he was. He was so proud of you, Finch. And now he would want you to pull yourself together and be strong for him."

Lilian's wails began to slow. Her breathing was coming under control, but her tears felt like they would never dry up.

However, Black was right. She needed to be strong.

Billy returned with a brown bottle full of rum.

"Here ye go," he said, handing the bottle to Lilian.

"I'm alright now," she said, refusing the drink and wiping her tears dry. "I think I'll go to the galley and get some water."

"I'll come along," Billy said.

"No, please. I'd like to go alone."

"Are you sure you're fine to go alone?" Billy asked her.

"Yes, I'll be fine," she said, as she stood and turned to face them. "Thank you all for your concern."

Her friends nodded as she ascended the stairs to the main deck – the last place she had seen her father.

Chapter 5

The sky had cleared after the intense ocean storm, and the sun was shining warmly on the main deck.

Lilian walked over to the railing where she had last seen her father. She placed her hands gently on the wooden rail and peered down into the sapphire blue water of the Caribbean. The sea was crystal clear, just as her father had said.

"I really can see the ocean floor like you said. I'm so sorry we couldn't look at it together."

As she gazed into the water, a school of colorful fish swam by and disappeared under the ship.

"Clown fish. I read about those," Lilian commented.

A single tear trickled down her cheek and dropped into the beautiful water below.

"Good-bye father," she whispered. "I'll never forget you. I love you. Always."

She turned away from the water and pulled her tri-cornered hat down over her eyes. Slowly and all alone, she descended the stairs to the lower deck where her and her father had slept next to each other for the past three years out at sea.

Her friends Billy, Black and Smythe had all departed the area. She was literally all alone.

She sat down on the edge of her cot and stared at the small bed where her father had slept just the night before.

Lilian reached over and took her father's pillow from his bunk. She kicked off her boots, took off her hat and lay down on her cot, clutching the man's musty pillow.

She closed her eyes and quickly drifted off into a restless sleep.

Chapter 6

The wind blowing through her long, wavy hair sent shivers down her spine. Not because the air was cold, but because of the freedom she felt in the ocean breeze.

Standing on the bow of her ship, she could finally be herself. Lilian Finch could finally remove her mask and let the world see who she really was.

Her long, beige skirt whipped around her calves as she turned from the water to observe her crew.

Five young women, all beautiful, strong and brave, helped sail the ship. One roosted atop the main mast in the crow's nest, two others washed linens in a tub set up in the warm sunlight and one directed the ship at its wheel.

Butterflies fluttered in Lilian's stomach as she gazed upon her crew. Pride filled her soul from head to toe, knowing she had a near perfect team of pirates sailing with her.

"Captain Finch," called the woman from the crow's nest.

"Aye. What see you?" Finch inquired.

"I see land, captain. About twenty degrees starboard," the woman reported. "Would ye wish to dock?"

"Aye," Capt. Finch commanded, and the ceremony of pulling into port began.

The crew of women worked as swiftly as cats, as graceful as doves.

In a flash, her ship was docked and two crew members were tying ropes to the dock pilings to secure the ship in the harbor.

"Ahoy crew!" Lilian spoke firmly, but sincerely. "You may go ashore. Be back when the sun be settin'. Fare thee well, friends."

Lilian watched the ladies leave her ship with pride and admiration. She herself would not be heading into town. She would stay with the vessel.

All alone on her prized possession, she let her mind wander back to her early days out to sea with her father and pirate family on the Blue Mist. How she missed him and those carefree days.

The refreshing breeze coming off the water in the harbor was perfect and the wake was just right to set her ship rocking lazily in the water.

"Finch!"

Someone was calling her name.

"Finch!"

But there was no one on board. She couldn't see anyone who would be close enough to call to her.

"Finch! Wake up!"

Chapter 7

Lilian woke with a sharp gasp.

She looked around. There were no other girls, no bright blue sky, and no ship of her own. Lilian was still on the Blue Mist, reclining on her bunk embracing her dead father's pillow.

"Sorry to wake you, Finch, but you've been asleep nearly ten hours." It was her good friend Billy. "You slept straight through the night, then the morning," he said, "and now it's nearly high noon!"

Had she really been asleep for so long? Just then she heard a rumbling sound. It was her stomach confirming that she had indeed slept through the night and morning – dinner and breakfast.

"You must be starving. Can I get you something?" Billy asked her.

Lilian swung her legs over the side of her cot and sat up, still clutching her father's pillow.

"No, that won't be necessary. I'll go and get something. I need some fresh air." Lilian told him.

"I'll go tend to my chores then," Billy told her as he walked off.

Lilian rose to her feet, setting the precious pillow down on her cot.

"Billy!" she called after her friend.

"Aye?"

"I'll see you later, ok?" she asked tentatively.

"Sure Finch!" he replied enthusiastically.

Lilian pulled her boots on and plopped her hat back onto her head.

She nodded to her friend, took one last look at the pillow on her cot, and headed for the stairs.

She was still grieving the loss of her father, her only family. But her dream – a premonition of her future – had inspired her and given her hope. Though she had portrayed the life of a young boy for 11 years, she knew it was time for a change.

It was time to be Lilian Finch – the sailor, the pirate, the girl.

Though she could not yet reveal herself, she could begin to make plans for her future. Plans that may involve leaving her extended family, the crew of the Blue Mist and also her best friend Billy.

But the strength and courage her father had instilled in her would help to carry her to new places, new adventures and a new world.

Lilian Finch would remain with the crew of the Blue Mist until she was ready to go off on her own. She would listen and learn and when the time came, she would leave.

Then she would commandeer her own ship, assemble her own crew and be off on her own explorations.

One day, whether it be soon or many years from now, Lilian would be known throughout the seas. She would be known as Captain Lilian Finch.

Chapter 8

four years later

"There looks to be an oncoming ship straight ahead, captain," Finch, now a 15-year-old, full-fledge pirate and top-notch sailor, called to Capt. Wellington.

"How's it look, Finch?" Wellington asked. "Be it friend or foe?"

Lilian stared into her spy glass and spotted the ship's colors. The flag was black, which meant it was a pirate ship. But who was it? Then she spotted the grinning skull hanging over two swords, crossed and plunged through a large, red heart.

"Sir, it looks to be Panama Pete and his crew," Lilian reported. "Orders, sir?"

Capt. Wellington didn't hesitate. He ordered his crew to prepare for what could turn into a battle.

Pirates were very territorial, even when out on the wide-open sea. Pirates always believed that the ships they encountered could be carrying better treasure then what they possessed themselves. Not to mention, pirates were always looking to add ships to their fleet.

Therefore, the approaching ship was a threat to the Blue Mist and her crew.

"Load the cannons!" the captain yelled. "Crew, get below until we know their intentions."

Finch ran below to help Black and Smythe with the cannons. This would be her first skirmish if it indeed escalated to a fight. She was a bit nervous, but also excited to defend her ship.

The unfamiliar vessel was approaching quickly. Finch peeked out the porthole in front of the cannon she had just helped fill, and saw the bow of Panama Pete's vessel.

"Where's Captain Wellington?" Finch asked Black, nervously. "How will we know when to fire?"

"Easy there, young one," Black said, trying to comfort Finch. "We won't fire unless necessary."

"You mean unless they fire on us, right, Black?" Finch asked.

"Aye, Finch. Now you've got it," Black confirmed.

Lilian concentrated on listening to the sounds coming from outside the Blue Mist. Everything was quiet.

Suddenly, she heard Capt. Wellington shout across the water to the other ship.

"Avast, Panama Pete," Wellington spoke to the captain of the opposing ship. "What be your intentions?"

"Simply sailing the open sea, Wellington," Pete said. "I've got no quarrel with the Blue Mist."

Lilian relaxed a little, thankful for the direction in which the conversation was going.

"On your way then, Pete," Wellington said, as he gave a congenial wave to Panama Pete.

Down below, William Black was not comfortable with the situation.

"Something's up," Black said.

"What say you, Black?" Sam Smythe asked his crew mate.

"Panama Pete's never friendly to other pirates," Black explained.

But Pete's ship continued sailing past without incident.

"He must be in a fair mood today," Lilian surmised.

"Aye crew, all clear," Wellington called.

Finch followed Black and Smythe up to the main deck to gather with the rest of the crew.

The sky was bright blue and the air was sweet and warm.

"We've a new heading crew. Turn about and sail due South," Capt. Wellington said.

"Where are we headed, Black?" Finch asked curiously.

"Back to the southern Caribbean, lad, the land and water of paradise," Black said, with a dreamy air about him. "And also the direction in which Pete be headin'. There's something out there he's after and we need to find out what it is."

Chapter 9

Two days and nights passed before the Blue Mist finally docked in the crystal blue waters of Sapphire Shoals.

The inlet was large and full of ships of all shapes and sizes. There, anchored on the outskirts of the shimmering harbor was Panama Pete's ship.

"Aye, there it is," Finch said, amazed. "We found him, Black!"

"As I told ye, Finch," Black said, with a slight chuckle. "Now we need to figure out why Pete and his crew were seeking this place."

Capt. Wellington led his men in bringing the Blue Mist into port, and then dismissed the crew to go ashore.

Lilian found her best friend Billy and the two left the ship to explore this new water town.

"Let's find Panama Pete," Billy, who's always looking for danger, pestered Lilian.

"No Billy. Let's just get a warm meal and get back on the ship," replied Lilian, who remembered all too well the time the two children had gotten themselves kidnapped.

"Come on Finch. We'll be careful. Wouldn't it be great if we discovered the reason Pete has come here to Sapphire Shoals?"

"No. It's not our job. Leave the spying to Captain Wellington," Lilian protested strongly.

"Fine," Billy said, as he started to walk away.

"Where do ye think you're going?" Lilian asked.

Billy ignored her and kept walking toward town.

"Fine," she yelled after her best friend. "But don't call on me for help. I already told ye not to go."

Lilian watched as Billy disappeared into the crowd.

"Ye daft scallywag," Lilian mumbled under her breath.

She went to find a tavern. She could really go for a hot bowl of stew or a hot beef sandwich. Even though it was warm in the Caribbean, Lilian rarely got to eat a warm meal while on board the Blue Mist.

She spotted a small café up ahead. The aroma coming from the small establishment was amazing.

Lilian had some money with her and decided to go in for a bite.

The café was small, but cozy. There were a few patrons, all sitting comfortably at small, wooden tables placed randomly throughout the room.

Lilian chose an empty table in the far back corner of the tiny room. Almost immediately, a young woman wearing a long, blue dress covered by a pale yellow apron approached her table.

"Good day lad, and what would ye like?" the young woman asked Lilian sweetly.

"Do ye have hot stew?" Lilian asked hopefully.

"Why would ye want hot stew on a fine day such as this?" the server questioned.

"Ye see, on my ship, we don't get many a hot meal," Lilian explained.

"Well, that I can understand, lad," the woman answered. "I'll see what we can whip up for ye."

Lilian thanked the woman, and the waitress headed for the kitchen.

This young woman in the blue dress and yellow apron was the first female Lilian had come in contact with since her days at home in Crown Port with Gabrielle, her care taker.

Talking to the young waitress made Lilian long to be herself. The night her father died, Lilian dreamed of shedding her disguise and becoming Lilian Finch, the woman.

However, no matter how much she longed for that freedom, Lilian knew she could not yet reveal herself. If she did so, she would be banned from the crew of the Blue Mist and would have nowhere to go.

Therefore, Lilian would continue the charade until she was ready to go off on her own – leaving behind the only family she had left – the crew of the Blue Mist.

"How's this, lad?"

The waitress had returned with a large, steaming bowl of hot oyster stew. The bowl was full of potatoes, carrots, celery and oysters in a creamy, broth base.

"Perfect," Lilian told the woman and smiled warmly.

"Here's some fresh squeezed juice and fresh baked bread to accompany your meal. Enjoy!"

"Thank you so much," Lilian replied, grabbing her spoon and digging in.

The stew was hot and tasty and definitely perfect.

Chapter 10

As she ate, Lilian watched and listened to the people around her.

There were men and woman, boys and girls and one very old man sleeping in a chair at a table near the front window of the café.

She found the conversations very interesting, even though some people would have thought the folks quite dull.

One couple discussed plans to build a pasture fence in their yard and purchase a few cows for milk.

A young boy and girl decided that when their parents finally left the café, they would head to the beach and take a dip in the lovely Caribbean waters.

The old man up front simply slept. His quiet snores and relaxed posture told Lilian this man had not a worry in the world. He was happy and his life content.

Lilian thought of her own life again. She had lost her mother before she even knew her, and recently lost her loving father to the sea. She loved sailing on the Blue Mist. She loved her friends Billy, Black, Smythe, Capt. Wellington and the rest of her crew mates. But she still longed for her real identity and her own life. She thought maybe soon would be the time to break away and become Lilian Finch, the pirate.

"How is everything?"

The young woman had returned to Lilian's table to check on her meal.

"This is wonderful," Lilian told the woman. "The best I've ever had."

"Glad to hear it," she said, sitting down at the one empty chair at Lilian's table. "So, ye sail on a ship, eh?"

"Yes, the Blue Mist. I've been with the crew since I was a wee lad," Lilian explained. "My mother died in childbirth, so my dad raised me up, and then took me to sea with him. It's my life."

The waitress looked fascinated.

"That's exciting, it is!" she exclaimed. "Where have you traveled."

"I've been all over the open sea, from north to south, east to west."

"How very exciting," the waitress said. "I've always wanted to sail the ocean blue. I just never had the opportunity."

Lilian was surprised to hear this young woman express her interest in sailing. Lilian had never met another girl who loved the sea as she did.

The waitress then reached out to Lilian. She had her hand outstretched. "My name's Storm, by the way. And yours?"

Startled, Lilian realized Storm wanted to shake hands.

"Oh," she said, grabbing Storm's hand with her own strong one, and shaking it firmly. "Just call me Finch."

"Nice to make your acquaintance, Finch," Storm said. She also had a firm grip, not light and wispy like most women. "So, where are your father and the rest of your crew?"

Lilian's smile began to fade. Her father was gone.

"My father died recently - taken by the sea in a terrible storm," Lilian said, her head dropping, eyes falling to look at the floor of the café.

"I'm so sorry, lad," Storm consoled Lilian. "That's a sad state, it is. And ye already lost your mum. What a sad state indeed. But I do know how ye feel, to a point. My parents are both gone, too. I've been on my own for about a year now."

"What happened?" Lilian asked.

"It was a sickness. They both caught the sickness and died quickly," she said sadly. "It never got me, but now I'm on my own."

"I'm so sorry," Lilian said to Storm. "It must be hard living on your own."

"Nay, I'm fine," she replied. "I've got my job and our little house and there are many people who I can call on if I need anything."

Lilian had lost both her mother and father, it was true. But she did have the crew. They were her family. The men on the Blue Mist protected her and taught her how to survive.

However, Storm seemed so different. Somehow, even though they had just met, she felt very comfortable with the girl. Perhaps it was because Storm was the first girl her own age she had actually sat and talked to at some length.

Lilian told Storm she was going to be all right. "The crew is my family now. I'll be fine."

"But you must be lonely sometimes," Storm questioned, "a lad of your age."

"I'm fifteen," Lilian cut in.

"Honestly? Ye look a bit younger. I'm fifteen myself," Storm told Lilian.

Storm was also fifteen. Lilian felt a pang of excitement at this discovery. Storm was a strong girl of fifteen who wanted to sail the sea.

Lilian had to wonder if Storm would want to be a part of Lilian's crew someday. In her dream, she had a crew of five young women sailors and they ruled the sea. Lilian knew one day this dream would come true. And now that she had met Storm, that day could come very soon; very soon indeed.

Chapter 11

After she had eaten every last drop of stew and every last crumb of bread, Lilian said good bye to Storm and left the café. She promised to keep in touch with her new friend, and hopefully come back one day when she could be herself, and ask Storm to sail with her and her crew.

But right now, she needed to find Billy. He had wandered off earlier. He was angry with her because she didn't want to face the danger of trying to find Panama Pete.

She guessed he would most likely be wandering around the docks, so she headed toward the harbor.

The docks were packed full of sailors, merchants, women and children visiting with their loved ones, but there was no sign of Billy. She glanced down the length of the dock and saw the Blue Mist bobbing in the water, waiting for her to climb back on board at the end of the day to set sail once again.

Not seeing Billy anywhere, Lilian decided to head back toward town to try to find her friend. She hoped she wasn't too late to stop him from looking for Panama Pete and possibly getting himself into trouble.

She passed a shoemakers shop and a saloon, a general store and finally the café where she had eaten her last meal and met her new friend Storm.

Further down the street, she saw a group of raggedy looking men. Some were drinking from large, pewter mugs and others were laughing loudly at one small, brightly dressed man in the center of their group.

The small man wore a bright red shirt, and bright yellow short pants belted with a green sash that was tied and hanging around his waist.

"Pete, ye can't just waltz up and take the ship, ye crazy rascal!" one of the dirtier men bellowed.

Lilian realized she was peering at Panama Pete and his crew. She decided to get a bit closer, just to listen in and see what she could hear.

As she approached, she saw one pirate who appeared quite a bit smaller and skinnier than the rest. He was just a boy and didn't seem to fit in with the group. When she got closer, she caught a glimpse of the boy's face. It was Billy!

She stopped dead in her tracks. What was he doing with them?! She had to get his attention. She had to get him away from those scurvy pirates.

Lilian approached the group of men, hoping her plan would work. As she walked toward the cluster of men, she began to whistle the tune of a song the Blue Mist crew always sang while working. She peeked up at Billy from under the brim of her tri-cornered hat. She saw Billy looking in her direction, so she motioned for him to come with her, away from those burly men.

He looked at her with a bit of fear in his eyes, and faked a laugh loudly for the others to hear. Slowly, and stealthily, Billy began to scoot behind one of the larger of the men, in an effort to get away from the group.

"Hey lad, where do ye think you're going?"

"Aye?" he said, with a bit of humor and a dash of fear in his voice. "Well, fellows, as they say in the business, nature calls."

The men all stared at him for what seemed like a lifetime.

Then suddenly, they all busted out into furious laughter.

"Aye son, that be true!" one pirate said, as he raised his pewter mug above his head.

Billy just grinned and easily slipped away from the group of men. Lilian turned back toward the docks and began to walk away. Billy soon caught up with Lilian and thanked her for her help.

"I didn't really do anything to get you out of there, however, you shouldn't have even been in that situation in the first place!" she scolded.

"I know that Finch, but I did find out why Panama Pete was being so kind to Captain Wellington," he told her. "He's planning to commandeer the Blue Mist!"

Lilian couldn't believe her ears. Steal the Blue Mist? How could the ship that had been her home for much of her life be taken right out from under her and the crew? There had to be a mistake. And if it wasn't a misunderstanding, she would definitely not allow Panama Pete and his men to take the ship where she had last seen her beloved father.

Chapter 12

"He can't take our ship!" Lilian said with conviction. "We'll fight him and his scurvy good-for-nothing crew!"

"Easy Finch," Billy said, trying to calm his friend. "We'll go find the Captain and tell him what I heard. We'll let him handle it from there."

Finch and Billy headed back into town to try and find Capt. Wellington and his crew. They guessed the men would be gathered at the saloon Lilian had passed earlier.

The captain, Black, Smythe and several other crew members were sitting at a large, rectangular table. Mugs, pitchers and plates full of food covered the wooden surface. The men were laughing and joking and having a grand time.

Finch hated to have to break up the festive scene, but Capt. Wellington needed to know Panama Pete's plan.

"Captain, may we have a minute?" Finch spoke first. "Billy overheard a conversation you need to hear about."

Capt. Wellington turned to face the children.

"What is it, lad?" Capt. Wellington said, placing a comforting hand on Lilian's shoulder.

"It's Billy sir," Lilian said to the captain. "He overheard Panama Pete talking about the Blue Mist."

Capt. Wellington looked at Billy in anticipation of his explanation.

Billy swallowed hard. He knew the information he had could start a battle between his crew and that of Panama Pete.

"Sir, I overheard Panama Pete telling his crew to prepare to commandeer the Blue Mist," he said hesitantly. "He said he knew you would follow him here and was planning the attack from the moment we encountered him out to sea."

Capt. Wellington pondered the information he had been given for a few seconds.

Suddenly, Lilian saw Wellington's face harden.

"Men, let's go," Capt. Wellington said as he stood and pushed his chair back hard. "To the Blue Mist," he commanded.

The men all stood as one and headed out the door of the saloon into the street. Their faces determined and their postures strong. Their attitude showed anyone who saw them that no one would be taking their ship today. Not today, and not ever, so they believed.

Chapter 13

Lilian and Billy joined the men in their march to the Blue Mist. Lilian was ready to fight. She was prepared to defend her ship. She had been taught that loyalty to her ship and crew was priority for pirates and she was determined to show her dedication in any way she could; even if that meant fighting to the death.

As Lilian approached the ship, she noticed a few men milling around on the dock near the Blue Mist. She didn't recognize the men at first, but as she drew closer, she spotted the bright red, yellow and green ensemble she had seen Panama Pete wearing earlier.

"That's him Captain!" Lilian said, running to catch up with Wellington. "That's Panama Pete. I saw him earlier."

"Aye, Finch, hang back," Capt. Wellington told her. "We'll need to approach slowly."

The men split up. Some went to the left side of the dock and some went to the right in the hopes of surrounding Panama Pete and the men who were with him.

Lilian and Billy ducked down behind two barrels, ready to jump in and assist when the action broke out.

Capt. Wellington stayed on a straight path toward Panama Pete. He walked slowly but unfalteringly forward. He pulled his tri-cornered hat down over his eyes in an effort to conceal his identity.

Before he could reach Panama Pete, Wellington saw the enemy pirate reaching for the thick ropes that held the Blue Mist to the dock.

"Pete!" Wellington shouted, pushing his hat back and lifting his head to stare at his opponent.

However, the rest of Panama Pete's crew was hiding on the dock, waiting for the crew of the Blue Mist to arrive and try to stop the operation.

Seeing what was happening, Lilian stood up and yelled to Wellington.

"Captain!" Lilian screamed and ran out from behind the barrel. "Behind you!"

But Lilian was too late. A large pirate with a huge metal pipe in his hand had emerged from behind a massive, wooden crate.

"No!" Lilian cried and ran after the man.

Suddenly, a dirty-faced man jumped out and grabbed her around the waist, stopping her in her tracks.

"Let me go!" Lilian struggled to get to her Captain.

All at once, the pirate, still holding Lilian around the waist, fell backwards, hitting the dock hard. The man landed with a thud and released Lilian upon impact.

Billy had jumped out from behind his barrel and pulled the dirty pirate down onto the dock.

"Run, Finch!" Billy shouted.

When Lilian got to her feet, she saw a brutal brawl occurring all around her.

Capt. Wellington was lying in a pool of his own blood. He wasn't moving. This couldn't be happening again. Not the

Captain! She had always thought of him as indestructible. Now she knew the truth – no one was indestructible.

She searched the crowd for her friends Black and Smythe. They were both engaged in a tough battle with Panama Pete's crew.

Lilian finally realized that she could not help in this situation. These men were all too big and too dangerous for her, and some were armed with weapons. If she didn't get out now, she could be killed.

She turned to get Billy. What she saw horrified her at once. Billy was lying still, half hanging off the dock. She ran over to him and pulled him back up onto the dock.

"Billy!" she yelled into his face. "Billy, wake up!"

The boy groaned and tried to open his eyes. He was alive!

"Don't talk. Pretend you're dead," Lilian told her friend.

She grabbed Billy under his arms and pulled him back behind the barrels.

"Lay here and don't let anyone know you're alive," she said. "I'll be back for you Billy, I promise."

Lilian peeked from behind the barrels and saw some of Panama Pete's men boarding the Blue Mist with her friends tied up, bleeding and crying.

She also saw Smythe trying to fight a mean monster of a man off of Black with not much success. Soon, two of her close friends would also be tied up, or, she feared, dead.

It was a blow out. Panama Pete's men had captured the Blue Mist.

Chapter 14

Lilian carefully snuck away from the deadly scene on the docks, in the hopes of finding someone to help. As tears ran down her face, she took one last glance at her friends and her ship. She saw a horrible man pick Billy up and fling him over his shoulder. The man carried her best friend onto the Blue Mist and threw him down onto the deck.

Devastated, she turned and ran. She ran towards town, hardly able to see through the tears streaming from her grieving eyes. She had no idea where she was going, she was simply running. She was running away from her life. She was running away from the sadness that seemed to be ever present around her.

Suddenly, she stopped with a jolt and fell to the ground. She had run right into someone. She shook her head to regain her bearings and looked up to see who had stopped her.

It was Storm, the waitress from the café.

"Finch! Are you alright? What's happened?" Storm was reaching down to help Lilian to her feet. She stood up slowly, eyes nearly blinded with tears.

"Oh, Storm! They're all gone! The ship, my friends, Panama Pete took the Blue Mist!"

Lilian collapsed into her new friend's arms.

Storm held Lilian tightly.

"Hush now lad. Let's get ye outta the street," Storm said, leading Lilian into a small shop.

Storm sat Lilian down on a wooden bench at the far end of the tiny shop and reached into her own pocket for a handkerchief.

She dried Lilian's tears and let the girl lean on her shoulder until she was calm enough to speak.

"Panama Pete ambushed the Blue Mist and her crew. I think Captain Wellington is dead and so are many of the others," Lilian said.

She stared into space for a long moment. She was breathing very slowly and felt a strange numbness growing inside her. She couldn't seem to snap out of her trance.

"Ouch!"

Lilian came back to reality when Storm smacked her gently, but forcefully on the cheek.

"Thank goodness, Finch. I thought I'd lost ye for a moment," Storm said, now rubbing the spot on Lilian's cheek where she had smacked her.

"I'm all alone now," Lilian said, beginning to cry again. "First, my mum died, then my father was taken and now my entire life is gone. I have no one and nowhere to go."

"Ah, now Finch," Storm said in a comforting voice. "Now, you have me. You can stay here with me in Sapphire Shoals."

Lilian looked up at her new friend, and managed a small, grateful grin.

"Really, Storm?" Lilian asked in a disbelieving voice. "You would take me in?"

"Of course," Storm said, matter-of-factly. "We are friends, correct?"

"Yes, I suppose we are."

Lilian suddenly felt her face go dull. Storm was indeed her friend, and she was glad the older girl offered to take her in at her time of loss.

But it finally hit her that she would not be going back out to sea on the Blue Mist with her crewmates. If she stayed with Storm, she would be tied to the land.

She had been at sea for so long that the water seemed like her home. Now, with the Blue Mist gone and her friends most likely either dead or prisoners of Panama Pete, she knew the only way she would get back to the water would be on her own ship.

Storm mentioned earlier that she had always longed to sail the open seas. Lilian finally realized the days of hiding her identity could be coming to an end. Lilian Finch, the girl, the pirate, would finally emerge.

Hopefully, Storm would be a part of her crew, and together the two girls would sail off in search of treasure, adventure and revenge against Panama Pete.

For a sneak preview of Lilian's next adventure,
turn the page and keep reading.

Lilian Finch: Captain at Sea

Book 1

Truth and Triumph

Chapter 1

Lilian Finch had seen much tragedy in her 15 years of life.

Her mother died shortly after giving birth to baby Lilian, her father had fallen overboard during a storm at sea when she was 11 and sailing with him, and most recently, the entire crew of the Blue Mist had been taken captive or killed, and the Blue Mist herself was commandeered by Panama Pete.

At one time, Lilian had a huge extended family. However, now she was alone except for her new friend Storm, whom she had just met in a café in Sapphire Shoals.

But when Storm heard about the ambush and discovered the Blue Mist had been stolen, she decided to take Lilian in and care for her as her own brother. However, Lilian was not a boy, and she knew she needed to tell Storm her secret soon.

As Lilian lay on the small cot in Storm's tiny house, she tried to plan how she would go about telling her friend her life-long secret.

Finally, Lilian decided the best way to tell her new friend the truth was to do just that – start from the beginning and tell the absolute truth.

Lilian rolled out of bed, slipped into her clothes, wrapped a square of fabric around her head and went out into the main room to find Storm. The older girl was busy in the kitchen cooking what smelled like bacon, eggs, potatoes and fresh baked bread.

As she approached the tiny kitchen, Lilian's mouth began to water.

"Smells great, Storm," Lilian said.

"Well, I hope you're hungry Finch, because I was in the mood to cook when I woke up this morning," Storm said, busily shuffling around the cooking area.

"Oh, I'm always hungry, you know that," Lilian said with a giggle.

Storm was finishing up and placing the steaming hot breakfast feast on serving dishes. The small table was already set, so Lilian plopped down in an empty chair.

"Make yourself comfortable, lad. Here comes your breakfast!"

Storm loved to cook and feed people, whether at home or at the local café where she worked as a waitress.

After the table was loaded with heaping plates of food, Storm took a seat across the table from Lilian.

Lilian had scooped up a plate-full of food, but had yet to eat a single bite.

"What's wrong, Finch? Why haven't ye eaten anything?"

Lilian looked up at her friend, but quickly dropped her eyes back down to her plate full of delicious food.

"Oh, no, something is wrong. Alright, Finch, let's hear it. What's the matter?"

Lilian knew that now was the time to reveal her secret. Now was the time to change her life forever. Now was the time to tell Storm, and the world, that she was a girl named Lilian.

She looked up at her friend, put her fork down next to her heaping plate and sat up straight in her chair.

She would start at the beginning. She would tell the truth, and she would pray that her friend would understand.

Lilian Finch: Captain at Sea
The adventure continues, will you?

CPSIA information can be obtained at www.ICGtesting.com
Printed in the USA
243672LV00006B/40/P